Contents

Preface

Poetry can bear the truest manifestation of genuine emotion. It is a mélange of past and future , of experience and prognostication, of reality and the absolute. Yet , rationality plays a major role in the creation of timeless poetry. An abundance of emotion devoid of reason may prove futile. Besides, the two opposing traits might be found in different kinds of poetry. Poems are sometimes intensely philosophical , and sometimes a mere versification of memorable moments in beautiful lines. Obviously the language of poetry nowhere comes near the language of everyday colloquialism. However, poetry is not bound to have prophetic or timeless theme every time. It can be very well about a recent event, either of local or international importance, or it might poetically comment on any public debate. Thus, besides its individualistic romantic approach to life, poetry can be public at times, circulated through newspapers or journals. Breaking the cocoon of poetic persona, it then gets involved in larger social, political or cultural issues. Nevertheless, the appeal of romantic poetry remained same to the readers for a very long time, as it embodies the deepest feelings of a human mind at a time of creative frenzy. Public poetry, since the time of Greek poet Pindar, has never replaced private poetry as the more popular kind of literature, but it has only aided to the variation and scope of poetry. I personally feel, the poet who can master both the forms of poetry, or it will be rather more preferable to opine that the poet who enjoys writing both for himself and for the society he lives in makes a complete poet. For me, as far as technicality is concerned, poetry can never be wholly confined to free verse even if people might argue we live in a modern world which best befits free verse for its fragmented nature. A poem written in free verse has its own rhythm or musicality. But a poem with rhyme and metre definitely has more of those dulcet faculties which poetry, for its inherent difference from prose, badly craves for.

In this book, I have accumulated the poems written by me during my second phase of young adulthood, the first phase obviously spent writing poetry predominantly in the European classical style, focusing on long narrative poems in archaic language. But here, I have written in a rather varied way, both in free verse and with rhyme and metre, thematically both private and socio-political. These are the poems I wrote during my days in the university from 2019 to 2021, despite being heavily affected by the pandemic. I hope sensible readers will not be disappointed after reading my works.

Sarban Bhattacharya
April, 2021

A Mythological Society

Before the air was flanked by 4G web,
And human energy at night would ebb,
The swift messengers only gods possessed,
Who loved to serve them, and did not take rest.
One Iris there was, whose celestial speed
Then no technology at all did need.
In lightning pace she reached this mundane earth,
Down swooping from the gods of divine birth.
And Hermes too wrought many a mischief,
With gifted speed he flew across a cliff.
No fake account in Facebook there had been,
But in disguise Zeus could the ladies win.
His status of relationship was same

As any married actor of great fame.
Beware! He had a furious fractious wife,
Who had the power to end those sweethearts' life.
Although Apollo was respectable,
He sported with the Muses desirable.
This society was quite similar to ours,
They only lacked computers and tall towers.

A Strange Day

I dreamt a dream of Rebecca,
As if she drew anear,
It was a dream filled with profound
Forgotten love and fear.

That was a joyful day I know,
We talked and played and sang
Within the spacious airy rooms;
Somewhere a church bell rang.

There all day long we ran and laughed,
And lovely words exchanged,
We plucked and ate our favourite fruit,
A wholesome lunch arranged.

Beside the casement long we stood,
And we beheld a stream,
Whose water made a ringing sound,
I heard in a sweet, sweet dream.

The evening breeze played with her locks,
That moved and swayed and flew,

And on her cheeks the moonbeams fell,
The evening breeze still blew.

She told me of her ancient home,
More ancient than this fort,
She could continue, unless a bat
would screech, her flow abort.

Down from the rafter he emerged,
Flew past the corridor,
His shiny eyes gleamed in the dark,
His flaps the silence tore.

We stood there still, we could not move,
A certain fume engulfed
Our eyes and mind, full numb we stood;
Meanwhile a wild hound barked.

I want to tell what happened then,
Although my brain betrays,
All the strange shapes men have not seen,
Did tame us and amaze.

A sudden noise, a ghastly noise
I heard, it broke my trance.
The buoyant soul of Rebecca
Off went, departed once.

Down from the terrace steep she fell,
She danced three years ago,
The sudden thud that ceased her breath,
Ceased her blood to flow.

Autumn Glides Away

There lies a way to heaven by that lake,
My sickness gone, I fear not chilly mist;
A redwing calls me, dawn is now awake,
The fragrant air smells of autumnal feast.

There is my home far from this cottage small,
Where honeysuckles with gold aspens mate,
And purple sweetgums love their mother Fall,
Oblivious of their harsh wintry fate.

November Rain! Your icy arrows smart
Those scarlet berries on the woody hill.
Let the thrush sing once more till I depart,
Let his mellifluous throat subtly trill.

True is this blazing arbour— October's art,
A timeless souvenir stashed in my heart.

February

Spring peeps through the door
Untimely rain imbues smoke
Smelling of burnt rose

Preparation for the Climax
A licentious night
Observes your succulent lips

Spilling wet pleasure.

Retribution

In sandy Egypt lived three men
In ancient days when pharaohs reigned
The kingdom of the pyramids,
Osiris and that Isis' den,
Whom everyone worships and heeds,
Or at least doing so they feigned,
And those gods too blessed them and deigned.
But these three men round whom my tale
Will be revolved, would surely fail
To get their blessings, but a curse
Of severe sort made their life worse.
They were young and licentious all,
They could not turn down Venus' call,
Which warmed their blood and wrought their fall.
Their mind oft groped for wealth and flesh,
Such cravings were a vicious mesh,
To which they found themselves entwined,
And this was the state of their mind.
Now summer hit Egyptian land,
They left their home and roamed about
Everywhere as a wanton band
To pirate, burgle, steal and rout.

Thus days went by until they found
A guiltless prey beside their home—
A widowed lady, sad and pale,
Her face was in deep sorrow drowned,
Bereavement made her weep and wail
Like a girl of a sorry dome

Whose eyes are full with briny foam.
She hailed from a rich family,
Still she could not live happily,
She had ample gold in her house,
But heaven took away her spouse.
This lady was such beautiful
That on her face grief could not rule,
But for her those three rakes would drool.
Thus once they broke into her room,
Till sable night there would they loom
Without her knowledge there they stayed,
And as she slept, therein forayed.
That night observed thunder and rain,
Whose sounds suppressed her plaintive cries,
When beastly men with might and main
Ravished her in a frenzied wise.

Thus they incurred Osiris' wrath,
The necromantic hell-bound god,
He cursed them with an evil spell,
And made them sail through briny froth,
And destined them to horrid hell,
For they had done a nasty fraud,
They tore a female rose unflawed.
They left her virtue wrecked and racked,
And stole her money which they lacked.
The greatest crime was not this though,
For which they should be sent below,
To tell of that requires a heart
Of stony kind or poisoned dart—
That night they did not soon depart,
But found a child witnessed their sin
And heard the noise of a sad din.
The rabid rascals out of fear
That they might be sent to king's peer,
Once the sad child revealed the fact
And with his mumbling tongue complained,

They could be jailed and badly whacked,
The wicked three their hands so stained.

The child lay lifeless on the floor,
His breathing ceased, his eyes were closed,
His little hands were trembling still,
He lay on his own ghastly gore,
His sobbing throat no more did trill,
His ruddy eyes forever dozed;
He was dead– all firmly supposed.
His mother touched his frigid hand,
As if it were a slender wand.
A drop of tear upon it fell,
Thereon the moonbeams glistened well,
A bloody child of a wronged dame
Should justly a strict vengeance claim,
And ease his mother's grief and grame.
A subtle fume came out his breast,
Flew past the saddened lady's waist.
It rose from an innocent tear,
So hallowed, crystalline and clear.
Like libations to holy beings
She sprinkled it on his pale face,
Whereby her wounded rage got wings,
It vanished fast lest one can trace.

To live with full impunity
The flagrant three men fled the state,
And readily embarked a bark,
All knew of their activity
How to purloin wealth they did lurk
In gardens, hills, oceans of late,
And how they stole a merchant's freight.
Their names were S and I and N,
They were accursed and caddish men,
Proud and nefarious were they,
They did refuse to love and pray.

As fate compelled them to sail through
The vast seas emerald and blue,
Whither to go they had no clue.
Osiris harried these three thus
As Neptune struck Odysseus
With thunder and great misfortune
And foul temptations opportune.
For six days they float on the sea,
And yonder saw a pleasant land,
The nearby isle did ever flee
Like an insect that flies one's hand.

There all at once something they felt
Beneath the boat whereon it stuck,
And thereby slowed its rhythmic pace;
It was a shore! Their eyes did melt
To find the land beside its base
Amid the gloomy marsh and muck;
Out of great joy they went amock.
It was a dark and pitchy night,
No evening star then offered light,
No polestar guided them ashore,
They heard the sea's deafening roar.
But that did not preclude the three
To wade and veer through wat'ry spree
Of marine waves, so fidgety,
Until they reach a monstrous house,
A castle which great fear did rouse
In the frail heart of any rogue,
And there ensued grim death's prologue!
'A mighty door, a mighty door',
One shouted to the other two,
'There is hidden as large a store
Of gold and flesh as we pursue'.

A lamp emerging from the dark
Implied the presence of a man;

A man! A man soon there appeared
From gloomy world and eerie murk.
His long and furrowed cheeks they feared,
And curly hair and forehead wan;
They thought he had an evil plan.
He wore a grey or blackish gown,
His eyes were bright, and nose was brown;
Those eyes emitted grisly glow,
Acquired from liquid lava's flow.
'Come hither', in an icy tone
He spoke, which froze their heart to stone,
Therewith they heard a lady's moan–
'Save me thou Lord, our potent Lord',
Her sobbing touched mind's inner chord.
And that strange man changed his grim shape,
His bright eyes changed to a child's gape.
A bloody child then there appeared
With his dead father and his train;
To them they one by one so neared,
And on the ground those three were lain.

The Political Fire

(A sonnet on the machinations of the Brazilian President Jair Bolsonaro, which
have prolonged the Fire of Amazon)

Such dream I had last night as people play
And dance on grey Amazonian land,
While Bolsonaro as their chief does pray
To boisterous devil with his wanton band.
They burnt the lively green-clad Nature's child,
Whose corpse eclipsed the Sun with ugly smoke;
On vast necropolis they all are piled,
And cover Earth with one miasmic cloak.

Good Macron's aid he scoffingly refused
For the 'development' of his large state;
'My farms and dams shall reign here'—he thus used
The unexploited verdant 'waste' of late.
    The war is cold, which won't extinguish fire,
When Earth will die, he'll play his deadly lyre.

The Sterile Movement

Between the eyes and on the temples,
the untold things in detail,
are engrafted in the language of pain,
sprung from the involuntary locomotion of thoughts.
The ghastly moments in horror stories I read
in childhood become innocuous and comforting.
They come and disappear into
the disorderly paraphernalia of guilt
and sinfulness, typical of the young minds,
embracing a horrific algorithm
spun around nights and days, and days and nights.
Very many things rave and rampage into there—
they knock and pull and strain and hurt
in restive sleep of howling gusts and gales.
How long will the storms numberless rankle it?
These are not futile cravings— cease,
CEASE the ruction of this smallest land, yet
as enormous as the volume of the universe;
moving or what?
Lull the sleepless pupils on the hearth, lead them
to the lush and tranquil island.
Is a fabled nowhere your resort? How will the
crumbling sinews react to this? I rose and found

a noisy market, where plies a train everyday,
vague and vacant.

Untitled Musings

1

I am alone at my home for a month,
for, I am sick, and I do not dare to go out,
I do not dare to frolick with her
who had made me smile.
But I have memoranda to live with,
a chocolate, and a few academic papers,
given to me by her,
which I do not use for consumption or
reading, but to soothe myself during
the time of cries and pains,
caused by the alienation from whom I love.
No, it is late,
it is late, and love is a train, which I failed
to board, and lagging far behind,
I see the other boys sitting comfortably
in its coaches.

2

Warm touch that leads to snuggle
and gentle rubbing in a cosy evening,
is remembered for its authenticity.
And thus you instigate in me
the primitive instinct of mankind.
and of the animal world that thrives
on such moments, characterised by
necessity, delicacy and pleasure.
In this adventurous journey,

you are the sailor, and I am a ship,
shaking, trembling, moving on the
storm-tossed ocean of the body.

3

You are wild and free, and
youth has given you freedom
to delight in sensual joy,
to break the chains of religion,
to have faith in the creed of insane lust,
to lie upon the chest of your favourite.
Yet deep inside you are bound,
just as me.
That which has give you freedom, and to
you too, has turned out to be
the instrument of stricture and slavery;
and our thighs are chained with
the verisimilitude of love.

4

He chopped down a leafy twig, grown upon the cornice stone, and the concrete
was as clean as a mirror.
A mirror bathed in rain reflects you, an image of a neurotic dream.
A gregarious group of schoolchildren shout on the street, and the mirror had a
crack, a very long crack.
They kiss and smoke and kiss and smoke as if in permissive France.
The balcony remains vacant most of the time, and I can go there till October chill
hurts arid lips.
The curtain's wet from the rain, for the window panes are off for repair, a shield
for noise and anxiety.

5

President Trump would disseminate the colours of Holi,
while the choking mouths are sprinkled with black, grey and white powders.
They rise and perch on the sleepy eyelashes,
and on the numb earlobes, reverberating the truthful rumour of
Li Wenliang's death,
Doctor Li's dead.
The words of liberty are manacled with golden chains, and the deafening noise of
a vibrant Indian
occasion smears the furrowed skin, lashed by the lurid hues of anguish.
The blue scars have suppressed a prophetic voice amidst dance and merriment.
Doctor Li's dead.

6

Weird smoke rippling above the newly replenished trashbin
Emaciated dogs scampering for food -
That is all you see.
Nothing happened since then, over the course of your journey.
The ferryman is busy doing the same thing,
his muscles stiffen.
Rough air filled his mouth with dust,
and you stared at him until you disembarked.
Did I too? His father had the same ordeal till he died.
The ferryman is nothing.
The sun sets late in some countries,
and the fading lights will confuse.

7

This is a world of silent conviviality,
spread across the tavern of mind,
where I see people seated on the
delicate sofas, waiting for someone to speak.
Their lips are moving, and the rusty
vocal chords are trying to emit
drab, repetitive words, to which
the immune ears are no longer sensitive.
I hear no words, which seem to be thrown into the void from the smiling,

tipsy faces drowned
in an enigmatic drudgery.

8

The library remains closed in the evening,
And the readers depart, and
The seminars too come to an end.
That is a common celebration of art,
And you are praised for your art.
The voices have faded now, they still
Reverberate in your ears.
Thereon you return to the universe,
Alone at night sans friends and admirers,
And hear your footsteps
Left behind you, gently tapping the numb
Repetitive breast of repressed ennui.
The library remains closed in the evening,
And no one reads.

9

New Year Eve
I see a sloshed face
Flushed with the warmth
Of processed French Cherry
Ruby lips talking of the unknown
With a pimple on the right cheek
Not covered up by concealer
Struggling to keep the hair
In order, conjuring up
Urbane wet pleasure
Of proleptic union
Hallucinatory

10

Reaching for that epicentre of bliss
Of transient and igneous nature,
Upon the toposheet of lusty skin;
Evoking the memory of atavistic instincts
Of mutual mission...
Reaching for your epicentre of bliss.

11

A tender nudge from you,
inadvertent though at a tedious seminar,
stole away the monotony thereof,
To thrust me into an effusion of thrill.

12

Flamboyant lights of the city
reflect upon your long-lashed eyes,
at the whirlpool of nocturnal revelry.
All the red and turquoise lights
are dimmed in a rhythmic frequency,
Corresponding to your dance steps
of spontaneous expression,
quintessential of the rapture of youth;
and the beauty of that bare shoulder
emerged in shadowy darkness,
defies the historic condemnation
of teetotaller fathers.

13

A vivacious evening--
resplendent light
haunts your neck,
while celestial beauty mates
with the tipsy lips,
craving for more.

14

If it be sin, let us sin together,
let us sin together amid the lush green,
surrounded by flowery thickets,
mysterious and fragrant. There I view
my lenient lady, unlike Diana, the overly modest and wrathful Greek goddess.
I listen to a sylvan melody,
while haply the leaves rub against each other; and over there a violent tigress
moans out of sensual
appetite.
Ah, let us sin, and empathise with her on this wet plane, at this moment
optimum.

15

Fill this palette, and generate
a synthetic colour, more gorgeous
than its components.
Paint a picture of sweetness on my skin
With those scarlet cherries, which are
a potential substitute of Picasso's brush.
It will turn into a picturesque
image on the canvas of my body,
for both my soul and yours are coloured in the same hue.
Upon the rough paper the process of
assimilation is pure.

16

Passion breeds pain, and Christ knew it,
and we call it the Passion of Christ;
Often California has wildfire in her
Beautiful pines and sycamores
for the regeneration of the green,
which possesses the holy energy
of singeing desire, coupled with rapture.
Therefore now I receive a wound,
Her lips seem red, tinged with blood,

The raspberries of youth.

17

Through the translucent mirror of rain
and grey ash, the city is observed,
thriving in its magnitude.
The reflection of my resuscitated mind
on the crystalline blessing of love,
resonates in the air of your world,
while upon the broken cornice
the unhappy popinjay will sing my song,
seasoned with the improbable tale
of my love, undisturbed by the
cacophony of traffic-- that long lost tale
of adolescent exploration sways
in the rhythm of rain.

18

Whispering into your mouth the theory
Of impartial love, suggests
Nasty and salacious adoration
Of temporal quality, unless it goes
Beyond the horizon of body.
And thereupon, suddenly,
I found the truth amidst a myriad of lies,
A momentary sparkle of truth,
As a hidden river beneath the ground,
Which, despite unseen , is still there,
And makes the soil fresh and wet.
The ways of preparation are manifold,
Which lead us to that overwhelming Peak of joyance.

19

The petal of your earlobe is undisturbed by the locks ,
as of Eve, whose nightly charm was

increased by stately Eden;
soft air and the fortunate surface
beneath you, are happy.
There your neck, half invisible, awaits a silent speaker on the skin.
No sound is heard, save a melody emerging from your mouth, unconscious, sweet
as a summer bird's song.
God is pleased to see us, His children, exultant, without transgressing His laws.

20

Let tonight be red,
red as a glowing conflagration usually is.
As a fiery meteor crashes upon the earth,
so these argent moonbeams kiss your eyelids,
and enkindle the fire of concupiscence,
which, for me,
is more psychedelic than the lunar bliss.
In you I observe my microcosm;
the sleek plateau of your forehead is
covered with silken strands of hair which
resemble the numerous tributaries of Nile.
Let me bathe in your scarlet cherries—
those lips whose waves are as graceful as
the breakers of Miami.
Tonight is short; before the vaporous clouds
blur the moon, let us explore
the mystic alleys of love; let the moon
teach us the craft of hallucination–
delirious sacred love, devoid of sanity
and composure, floats on the turbulent
current of Atlantic, without a destination.
Can we forget the bounds of superego?
Transcending the stagnation of mind and soul,
take me all the way with you,
to the utopian paradise, that we may
resemble the first parents of mankind
before they were unashamed of their nakedness.

And you, my Eve,
with you I crave to savour
the senses, the gustatory exhilaration.
Thus with the language of silence,
ah, singe our desire, gifted by God,
without transgressing His mandate.
Close your eyes, fade into an inebriated trance;
from the burnt ashes of love, a new Phoenix will rise.

21

Scribbling life everywhere may redeem
your composure.
Will you look at the trees beneath which
nestles love, beyond the newly dyed wall,
battered by dust and smog?
Her leaves stoop from half-died boughs,
children of a tree dripping bloody fluid
downwards.
You are feverish without a fever,
such a febrile malady has touched
your mind, an invisible wand that takes
you to the world unknown.
No one is there;
that is a pale and desolate ground.
Is anybody there?
There you must move to an incredible land
of mist and peace, an air of mild rest.
the perennial agitation we kill;
determine the day of its death, because
no longer one requires those precarious
impediments to the flourishment of life.
Pricking sensibilities run over me,
that is how something rankles people.
Happy children are they, you measured
their happiness with segregated nerves.

The Dying Rose

The rose can't brave the strength of agile time,
Which thwarts her pride and takes away her grace;
She harbours hope to rise in a new clime.

The rose had scoffed at that yonder wild thyme,
For it was not endowed with a svelte face;
The rose can't brave the strength of agile time.

When she was youthful, nature sang a rhyme,
The vernal wind wanted her sweet embrace;
She harbours hope to rise in a new clime.

The rose envies the oak, whom she can't mime,
That tall tree defies time's unceasing race;
The rose can't brave the strength of agile time.

God forgives time despite his vicious crime,
That hapless, transient rose he would deface;
She harbours hope to rise in a new clime.

One single rose —a special paradigm—
Is trounced and tarnished by time's lightning pace.
The rose can't brave the strength of agile time,
She harbours hope to rise in a new clime.

A Stream

There was a fountain in an African desert.
Long ago it ceased to exist for the tropical heat,
But its subterranean canals were intact;
And one day, when the earth was hot indeed,
The dry surface of the ground panted like a mare.

There came a storm, a tempestuous storm and rain,
Which drenched the thirsty trees, and rejuvenated
That geyser fountain, gushing forth above the ground
Like a vigorous jet of hot water to satiate the soil,
Again and again, for it was suppressed for long.

An earthquake shook the plates under it,
Aftershocks poured in— violent tremors, which
Continued to shake the ground up and down
Until the fountain gathered more strength, and flowed
To disappear into a holy cave of enormous pleasure.

From there arose a new being, a fresh new being.

The Miseries of the Mind

Listen to the sobbing air, smothered by
a satanic blanket of carbon monoxide.
Condemn me not, though I may be impatient,
for my wishes are aborted under industrial waste.
Weave your glowing tapestry of life; believe me,
I won't touch your creation lest it be tarnished,
permit me to view the process of your creation,
so pure and divine, which, my moribund mind
will observe silently, in utter seclusion.

From the realm of rustic serenity, far from
all urban ructions, the insomniac nightingale makes
a last call for lonely hearts, that resonates
in the mind of broken delirious people in a tavern.
My dream is another version of reality.
My love is alive, injured and bleeding unceremoniously.
I suppress the sound when it writhes in pain,
stabbed by the fruitless cravings for affection.

October Beckons

With mild rays the Sun does snuggle me in this breezy morn,
Oh Earth, forget your imminent wintry woes, as Fall placates you,
She gives offerings of raspberries and vines of gorgeous taste,
The senile year will make you moan with inebriating bounty,

Oh Earth, forget your imminent wintry woes, as Fall placates you,
Benignant nature has set ablaze the crimson maple today,
The senile year will make you moan with inebriating bounty,
My desirous mind seeks solace in nature's succulent arms,

Benignant nature has set ablaze the crimson maple today,
She gives offerings of raspberries and vines of gorgeous taste,
My desirous mind seeks solace in nature's succulent arms,
With mild rays the Sun does snuggle me in this breezy morn.

The Flavour of Spring

Winter is gone now;
Small buds in Earth's womb,
With their red, blue heads,
Proclaim she's pregnant

After a long time.

Mating with sky,
And April rain,
She derives joy
In giving birth.

Fertile smell,
Sweet and mild
Pervades me.

Eyes touch
New leaves,

Dozed.

The Crescent Desire

The mind is perturbed by the spiritual restraint
of the senses; what will the crescent desire do?
The nimbus clouds may kiss themselves and disperse temporally, before the
violent pressure pours.
How will you moisten your soul— after the manner
the droughty ground imbibes rain?
To feel a splash on the eyes at a heated afternoon,
I drooped my eyelids, disabled my vision,
and restrained all the senses with the exception
of tactile pleasure— the electrifying friction of your lips moving as a pendant,
gently brushing through
the carnal contour of my unexplored zones.
In the evening, the nimbus clouds will gather again,
but they may not postpone the outburst.

A Lover's Grievance on Valentine's Day

On the pleasant day of Saint Valentine,
With ardent love sly envy ambulates,
Which makes the mystic ways of love to shine
In lovers' mind that cautiously oft mates.

Love februates the rusty mind today,
The crimson eyes exhume forgotten tales,
Defying the onward march of time they stay,
While din and revelry subsume my wails.

I drowse in the mellow Camellia grove,
These purple daphnes kiss my moistened cheek,
They lull me while in distant woods I rove;
The fragrant fumes trance me and make me weak.

This moonlit night and thickets serve me wine,
They wipe my tears for long-lost Valentine.

Note that 'februate' means 'to purify'. February is conceived as a month of purification.

Sacred Love

These lonely hours amble in turtle's pace,
And hurt my mind with grief's untamed inflow;
Now all but me are blessed with Cupid's grace;
He hurls his darts from skies and glides below.

I too was once struck by his honeyed blow,
Her image I bear with me all the time,
Like dearest plant I water it and grow,
It thrives and blooms in my heart's doleful clime.

How can one love another human being?
All are destined to pair with universe.
Clay brings forth only clayish offspring,
Nature takes love from earthly things diverse.

My grief, these vernal shrubs alleviate,
And with my heavy heart they copulate.

The Ballad of the Forsaken Lover

My fairest damosel, you sing a lay,
The way the Philomel released her voice,
From pensive throat in breezy summer day,
That best behoves a lover's futile choice,
My fairest belle, prithee, you sing a lay .
You will marry another handsome swain,
Good bloke indeed to break a fragile heart,
The shades of maple know our amity,
Blessed hours of noontide in that cool sojourn,
Your brawny love received not Cupid's dart,
He brandished it to me with certainty,
A tingling ache with itself it has borne,

And let me down with its incisive art.
We count the stars in serene midnight skies,
A world of mystery void of any lies.
Memory loves those days at verdant lawn,
A sweet remembrance of the woebegone.
Far, far away I heave my covert sighs,
Whence a sad stare did strain the morbid eyes.
The bloated clouds cry in the month of May,
My fairest bonnibel, for once you sing a lay,
And in my heavy heart may hold your dulcet sway.

Valediction

Now far away thou must from mine eyes go
For studies' sake, naught will impede thy prise;
But in my tender heart my love shall grow
Like a huge Oak that day by day doth rise.
What can dissuade thee from thy noble wish
To serve the daughters Nine of Father Jove?
I warrant that my love won't diminish,
The while thou too mayst cherish our sweet love.
And when thou wilt return to native shore,
As wise as any rhetor, I shall find
Thy long absence hath my love deepen'd more,
And thine as well that mayst not change thy mind.
    As purest gold is tried in wrathful fire,
    So Love is tried by Time's wheel, swift and dire.

Notes:

Naught :Nothing.

Prise : Enterprise, the noble enterprise of my ladylove to study abroad.
The daughters Nine of Father Jove : The Muses, who hold sway over various
domains of art and studies.

Composed on My Birthday, the Twentieth Day of May

Thou gentle May that barest me one day,
Thou month of loveliness and darling flowers,
Didst fill mine heart with gaiety when I lay
Upon the cradle in my home for hours.
There in the yard I heard my mother speak
Of faery lands, of Queens, and of the Kings,
While yonder verdant heaths and Birches meek,
With breezes sway'd that to my ear still rings.
Think of the days when lovers make the best
Of their fond wanderings by sunny vales,
And flowers and fragrance of the arbour-breast,
Please e'en the belle that for her husband wails.
   With such a natal day thou mad'st me blest,
   When woes bygone and hung are nuptial nests.

Notes:
Barest : Archaic form for 'bore', past tense of 'bear'.
Faery: Archaic spelling of 'fairy'.

The Burnt Chateau of California

(A Mythological Interpretation of the Glass Fire)

Apollo rides the chariot of the Sun,
Full gay and melodious is his song,
September halts his wain and stops its run,
The dying summer dupes Apollo's throng.

The Muses follow him and love his lyre,
But they are jaded by Sun's gloomy rays,
While Bacchus, god of wine, fumes with desire,
In Chateau Boswell spends his tipsy days.

His turquoise eyes and corrugated hair
Attract the frenzied ladies to a sport,
A game of youthful passion in his lair,
Which makes Apollo envious of some sort.

The Muses have forsaken long his trail,
While his half-brother danced with ladies' train
In the plush grapevine of the Napa vale,
So well nourished by Californian rain.

Apollo brandished thus his bow one day,
And aimed a burning arrow at the green,
From Helicon he launched his lethal flay
That kindled thunderous fire unseen.

The serpentine flames poached the Rose's life,
She dropped her charred red petals in death-throe,
While the vineyard that the other day was rife
With purple grapes, is struck by a god's bow.

The elixir is dead and now forlorn
Within Boswell, smouldering, effete,
What if a new hope springs from death, reborn,
From nature's cradle yielded to defeat.

Sonnets

1

Five years have passed since last I saw that smile,
When childhood left the beauteous ground of life,
A mellow change walked on the body's aisle,
A boulevard with blossomed cherries rife.
With growing eld first-ever joys are gone,
No more I see you often as before,
Yet somehow I have learnt to carry on,
If faint hope fails, nonchalance can restore.
No shades even peeped on my woeful cheek,
I am ensconced in claustrophobic rooms,
Here memories flashing by appear so bleak,
That in subconsciousness frail pleasure dooms.
Now patiently I'll wait for your rebirth,
From relics old I glean both grief and mirth.

2

My dearest one has long forsaken me,
And faded in the fog with fluffy hair,
A mystic arras caused pale agony,
Of how my tattered clothes don't have a glare.
Once those were painted like the vernal leaves,
Fondled in the embrace of purple flowers,
Around which moorhens craft their reedy weaves,
With all the filial love in swampy bowers.
There do I whine in unknown misery,
Delusion here preceded further woe,
When angst and fear rule out affinity,

And play spoilsport for wielding Cupid's bow.
A fleeting youth nimbled by anxious nerves,
Rewinds not time it fatuously serves.

3

Deeper have I inhaled the smell of leaves,
Sprung on the boughs of shady midnight pine,
My rooftop's been embraced by verdant sheaves
Of clustered plate of nature's soulful shrine.
The dull electric light restricts my sight,
Put out the vestige of forged artifice,
The astral glimmer steals a lover's plight,
Derelict heart through murky interstice.
For how long would this mellow dream prevail,
Ere morn invades the town with vapid noise?
In southern gales my rippling hair sets sail,
Visions pass of her old days' amorous ploys.
The moist skin of the new-blown tuberose cries
The dripping dew of petals of my eyes.

4

Grim silence may diffuse a frozen tie,
Old rusted amity reduced to naught,
Sad tale of solitude and dreamy lie
Impede the golden sunshine once I sought.

Rain clouds weep off their vaporous offspring,
Cool torrents take away my dearest pain,
And molten shadow of her wedding ring,
An unseen relic born to April rain.

What for uncanny hope betrayed my zeal?
Delusive damsel faded at the dawn,
When stormy night would cease her gusty peal,
That shakes my window pane and raids the lawn.

Crushed are all wishes when fate plays a game,
And leaves me bound in painful memory frame.

5

To whom shall I declare my truest faith,
When 14th knocks on layman's humble home,
Bewitched by cruel Cupid's loveless wraith,
That stops me from exploring Kubla's dome?
I pray thee, thither journey we along,
To find the best essence of amity,
We both shall sing the choicest Yorkshire song,
And dance on beats of juvenile levity.
Can there be not a moment of respite,
From the coarse ailments of the sullen town?
A sudden truce to the never-ceasing fight,
Nor cherished end to the pain of a clown?
Carry me through all these bits of joyous frames,
And lift my spirit to the highest flames.

6

Encumbrance can affect in various ways,
To disallow me seek your company,
From which my age prevents me and betrays,
And forge a different sort of amity.
Entangled in an ambivalent maze,
Affection dwells in needless naivety,
Instead of love, in mind confusion plays,
With grave concerns reduced to levity.
But everything is solved if you agree,
Your luscious beauty grows with honeyed eld ,

And wisdom deeper, oft enchanting me,
The rift of time and age will soon be felled.
Then your sweet voice will resonate right here,
In my heart purged of shame and blushful fear.

7

As time refines the vintage Highland wine,
So it exalts your poignancy of grace,
That never ceases to glimmer and shine
Towards perfection in an endless race.

I know your beauty is concocted thus,
With wisdom mixed as in a proper blend,
That boasts a rendezvous of purest class,
And gives a frenzied pleasure at the end.

Who cares about the aching heart of his,
That's struck by something unattainable?
It offers me a tempting short-lived bliss,
When I stare at your eyes inscrutable.

My fate has long bereaved me of the joys
That your mere presence in the heart deploys.

The Arrival of Bacchus

Tonight a god descends with rare design,
The thick-plumed finch does squeal for his advent,
A merry god he is, prince of the wine,
To heal the laymen of their long lament.
Cheer on, deserted lads and maidens fair,
Untie your flowing hair, and let it soar

And sweetly flutter in the perfumed air,
Unleash your chains, and dance on grassy floor.
Let no constraint malign your youthful gait,
Our princely god is as you, she and I,
He knows not judgement, anger, grief and hate,
He is a god as you and she and I.
Enkindle the bonfire around the groves
Of flavoured grapevine filled with piquant fume,
A floral bodice might replace the robes,
Don't vacillate, a divine spree resume.
He brought a vessel to confine this spring
In luscious berries sparsed with crimson rose,
No moral shackle can preclude you sing
Today the song of rain and mystery shows.
The time has now arrived, forget the sting
Of fear and hatred for the fancied foes.

Another Version of Numbness

Exhaustion brings forth emotional happiness,
Ephemeral drug-induced exhaustion gives time enough to recall what is lost
during the noisy turmoil of cobwebby mind.
Silent is the room, a round robust room,
safely peregrinated around by Ferdinand Magellan.
I imagine how impeccably resilient is the barrier – a bony barrier of body contains
an intermittent ruction,
the turbulence of nothingness.
Then comes a thin cutaneous membrane all over the body, potent to conceal an
absolute abyss.
Envy does not provide with comfort.
A spiffing news spreads faster than rumour. Here I sit, sleepy and carefree, to
imbue my vein with your pleasure. The pleasure of the universe attacks and
multiplies like a contagious disease; An opaque streak of burnt hope appears,
disappears,
disappears and appears in the guise of pleasure, whom we craved.

It's nothing more than a deceptive premonition of healing.
Let him convalesce who is meek and naive. These be my final words before
another fit of unknown trepidation begins.

Anxiety and Escitalopram

Let me make a plan of it,
Whether or not to utilise the time
Before it starts off again,
The sudden feat of descension
Into the abyss of numbness.
Let us make a plan of it,
Whether to rewind the reel of time,
And retrieve the joy of new-found life.
Let me be quick, and you too,
For longer I cannot ponder upon the joys,
It hits me back with precarious attacks
And deepest breath of unknown fear.
A momentary prospect of happiness
Takes away the simplest of pleasures,
With fear unknown.
You are the most beautiful,
You are implored to make a plan for me
When the SSRI reigns in the brain
For a transient period, so that your perfume
Might emancipate me
From this vicious gyre of ravenous angst,
Leading the tired neurons toward
Peace and tranquillity.

Political Observations

The Forgotten Saga of Donald J. Trump,

An Incarnation of Agamemnon or Atrides, King of Greece.

Great Atrides was hated by the Greeks,
Achilles wrangled with him for some weeks.
But well he knew King Agamemnon's power,
He could return unscathed to his own tower.
So Don J. Trump fell out with leaders vain,
Who grabbed for long GOP party's rein.
When hypocrites spread lies about the state,
And joined hands with the radicals of late,
Then Don emerged from Agamemnon's ash,
To find the truth of World Trade Centre Crash,
And endless wars in middle Eastern lands,
From Iraq to the Arabian sands,
Alleged by Barry and the Clinton's hoard,
As crooked as Patroclus's worshipped Lord,
Achilles, who had gone against his King,
For ego and his narcissistic sting,
Like renegades within Republicans,
Like Romney who detests Americans,
And all the values cherished from old age
He nullifies with Democratic rage.
False propaganda thus were preached around,
And media were by leftist shackles bound,
During the eight-year regime of false hope,
That to the people was offered like dope.
Then all at once like a great Greek hero,
Arrived a man with weal and wealth's halo,
To purge the nation of all miseries,
To save it from leftist skuldeggeries.
Now all the knaves of nasty politics

Began to hate him just like fanatics,
Within his own and opponent party,
For they all feared their lives in jeopardy,
For all the crimes wrought with impunity
Won't go unpunished was a certainty.
Like Atrides he held his country first,
So he was by the opportunists cursed.
They ousted him to continue their sin,
And took away from him an obvious win.
But he shall reign in people's heart always,
He will be remembered for many days.

V-day, Nay Nay

The lovebirds like to lurk beneath the tree,
Unless a neighbour pries upon their spree.
But be certain no ravens check out it,
Instead of lips, you'll end up eating shit.
The crows are the best voyuers, I have heard,
Out of envy they'll play their shitty card!
If you prefer a park, please sit on ground,
The benches might not be quite strong and sound,
A fall might hurt your amorous prospect,
If suddenly you break your pen erect.
Be careful of the whitely clad cops too,
In secret bush or groves their sticks pursue.
No-parking zone claims fine of costly sort,
But no-kiss zone can lead you up to court!

On the Intrusion of Foreign Celebrities in the Matter of Farmers' Protest in India

(Written after Greta Thunberg and Rihanna made provocative remarks on farmers' protest that tried to violate the sovereignty of India)

There was a time when people had all tasks,
And tilled the fertile ground without these masks.
In Vedic age the Indians were so proud
Preparing paddy fields they themselves ploughed.
Yet none complained of little rain they got
In drier months, nor blamed their pallid lot.
Some carried same traditions very well,
Some not, and from the grace of nature fell,
Wherefore the ancient kings could harbour peace,
The kingdoms great need subjects great iwis.
Else harmony can anytime be breached,
By foreign powers the state can be besieged.
Invaders sniff a schism here and there,
They fail if only it's a tiger's lair.

An Eastern Sage: Prime Minister Modi

The beard of wisdom, since Socrates' days,
Hath given a great trouble to phoney dissenters.

Greek and Vedic seers
With symbolic facial hair
Can pierce the truth unknown to laymen.
The legacy of Aristotle , of Plato and Sophocles,
And in the East, the greatest epic poets , Vyasa and Valmiki,
Conquerers of highest knowledge,
Is carried by the Prime Minister,
A true statesman.
His oratory behoves the white beard, words of peace and wisdom,
Unintelligible to decadent Congress ,
And her sycophants galore,
Useless stashed in store,
Within the glorious parliament,
Who deserve an outright excommunication,
For their deceptive prevarication,
Led by the example of an Italian lad,
Of whom the greatest flatterer is a 'Sassy' man,
Pompous and old, mumbling a myriad of rare English words, in no order, jumbling
and tumbling, and ruining the beauty of the language.
The glorious Prime Minister shall reign,
In the land of history and piety ,
Defying many an adversity,
The one true voice ,
Amongst a host of spurious intellectuals and envious demagogues.

Trump Tower

Upon a concrete frame and limestone base,
Lo there, the vitreous building arose
Surpassing all in height from Raegan's days,
Whose mere sight does great awe and wonder pose.
A world of luxury and visual joy
Might overwhelm people who enter there,

And make their mind with Der Scutt's brilliance cloy,
While at this beauty jealous Dems may sneer.
Yet they can't but look at its lofty peak
That cleaves the bosom of the New York sky,
As though defying socialists' nasty trick
To halt American dream from soaring high.
Its gilded walls and lavish outlook slay–
The tower of hope and Presidential sway!
— — — — — —

(Der Scutt was the chief architect of Trump Tower)

A Merry Wish

If I were born beside the River Thame,
My father had a 'Lord' beside his name,
My mother called a 'Baroness' by all,
I could be there in the Westminster Hall,
As a part of the British government,
An MP fond of joy and merriment,
A young and vibrant man of politics,
An exponent of art and aesthetics.
I could know how the Chivas Brothers' wine,
Of malt is made, and renders all divine!
From nineteenth century it draws its taste,
When Chivas brothers built their store in haste.
Before Queen Victoria took the throne,
One William Teacher in all his glory shone!
He made a vow to find an unknown taste,
And scoured the Scottish highland in all haste.
His passion was no less than Columbus,
His research was a tipsy omnibus!
More malt he used to show his wondrous feat,
And sober men cried out, 'tis bittersweet!
I must not digress, and my dream recall,

Although fictitious, I may tell you all.
Then English Island bubbled with the zest
To sail through sea and undertake no rest.
I dreamt I had a friend of noble birth,
Who in romantic poems found his mirth.
He was a member of the House of Lords,
And fought mock-battles with his puny swords.
On battlefield of London's shady parks,
He, as a knight, with cute warriors lurks!
His father knew not of his bold exploit;
In bloodless battlefields he was adroit!

On the Great American Ideals of President Donald J. Trump

The President has shown us how to fight
In frontal war against the fiercest foe,
Be it a virus or a sudden plight,
Not flinching back in fear like craven Joe.

Like Trojan Hector he holds his country first,
And puts his life at stake to preach the truth,
How 'saviours' of working class had cursed
Their lives with shipping jobs abroad in sooth.

He prefers not to swerve from national tasks,
He hates the plague, but loves the common breed,
Unlike that man who wears the 'biggest masks',
To save his face from flu and past misdeed.

No wonder they have vowed to shut the nation,
And halt economy for good herein,
As anarchists hold violent demonstrations,

Deluded by their socialist leader's sin.

While they keep men obsessed with Wuhan flu
And factious protests, promising utopia,
The general mass gets poor without a clue
In blue-capped liberals' black dystopia.

The chilly night of darkness once will pass,
Brighter the crimson sky of joy will glow,
St. Matthew said, kind Jesus will heal us,
The gold-haired President will trumpets blow:

Trumpets of peace and glory in a morn,
A dreamy dawn with no disease and fraud,
American dream he craveth to adorn
With bounty, unity and grace of God.

Nancy Pelosi's Hanky-Panky

(On Nancy's visit to a salon, violating Covid restrictions)

There's no age bar on titivating hair,
Apart from putting rouge on wrinkled cheek.
A Speaker has the right to looking fair,
And prune her brunette hair once in a week.
Pandemics come and go, but beauty stays.
At eighty, beauty makes a second wave
When handsome youngsters leer at granny's ways,
And to impress her get a cleaner shave.
Though she may ask us all to wear a mask,
It must not hide her young and rosy lips,
Or smudge her makeup if she wants to bask
In TV lights with hair like fresh tulips.
She can do nothing wrong, she is the queen
(Of two-faced bitches who are shrewd and mean.)

The Fisherman's NET

(NET or National Eligibility Test is a nationally conducted exam in India to recruit lecturers and professors)

There goes an exam by the name of NET,
Which picks professors very wise, I bet!
By hurling bombs of MCQ on screen,
Like tiny babies in need of a wean!
And as they crawl in all fours on the floor,
These four options open the sacred door
For colleges which harbour brilliant brats,
Who blabber all like buzzing market gnats!
It goes on for a longer time you know,
Than antique rivers from the mountains flow.
If vehicles are not there, you trust yours legs,
To reach the halls, exhaust yourself to the dregs.
But if you shine on holy exam's day,
You will receive salvation straight away!

On the General Secretary of CCP

Do raise your voice, ensure Xi Jinping's fall,
Before mankind confronts his nasty strike,
Resist the kingdom where the devils crawl
With Covid-19, SARS flu and the like,
Do expedite Communist China's fall!

All brothers of Europe and Asia, rise
Against the biggest threat of humankind,

The Soviet Union's ghost in China lies,
And plots our death that haunted Stalin's mind,
Now save the world and cause Jinping's demise!

Forget love-letters, flowers and Keatsian lines,
Bygone are days of sweet and rounded verse,
For human values day by day declines,
And China fights in the disguise of Marx.
But O behold, our victorious emblem shines!

We will repel Xi Jinping's Shameless claim
In the South China Sea and Indian land,
Retaliate, or soon he will rename
This world as Greater China as he planned,
Like Mao he seeks to gain notorious fame.

Prepare at once, don't vacillate to slay
The greatest demon of the present time,
Put on your armour and do not delay,
Let us reduce him to the muddy slime,
Where with the viruses on Chinese clay
He and his comrades wriggle for their crime,
Or let them starve severing business ties,
Your wrath is latent, vent it and arise!

A Tribute to Prime Minister Modi

All hail the stabber, stabber of the foes,
He will avenge the martyrs with harsh blows.
The Chinese kingdom fears his thunderous voice,
Save going backwards they don't have a choice.
O hither comes the menace of the foes!

Within his veins the blood of India flows,
Blood of a war, not of a crimson rose,
For these are times of howling horrid wars,
Don't while away your time by counting stars.
All hail the King, the killer of the foes!

A foreign race of disease-spreading beasts
Assaulted us, and used deceptive tricks.
Our King has now unsheathed his shining sword,
Deployed the troops, who guns and cannons stored.
Replace life's poetry with sturdy prose,
All hail the ripper, ripper of the foes!

Another Tribute to Prime Minister Modi

Please boycott China and don't oppose our King,
Twice with the mandate people brought him in,
Xi Jinping trembles, trembles at our King,
The whole world loathes Xi's catastrophic sin,
Support our sovereign, benevolent King!

He brandished arrows to the demon's breast,
Those sacred arrows which Lord Rama held
To tear apart a Lankan Monster's chest,
Against our holy Mother he rebelled.
Lo, cometh here our King of broadest breast!

All farmers, labourers and friends arise,
A foreign danger hangs upon our head,
All Indians, poor or rich, do hurl your cries
Of joy and victory without a fear or dread.

Let us of his victorious chariots sing,
All chant the glory of our valiant King!

Equality

To the state, Lilliputian all men are,
Equal in wealth, which Marxist regime boasts,
And no distinctions their discomfort mar;
Ambitious men are frowned and punished most.

Men worship Poverty, she is divine;
Rich magnates, who give jobs, are demonic.
Religion is evil in Leftist shrine;
All frenzied revolutions are beatific.

Conformism— oh that is quite dated now,
Sophistication's hateful, drug means trend,
Churchill's bad, for he saved the world, you know;
With violence Castro and Mao themselves defend.

Thus socialism benefits society—
I am safe here, for Stalin is my deity.

Subversive Modernism in Art

'Progressive' mind accompanies the art
Of writing poetry at present time,
Great intellectuals from all forms depart,
And love free verse that spurns metre and rhyme.

If poems be composed in such a way

That lines consecutive are relevant,
They may attract the readers' rage today
As they convey what they have truly meant.

Why should not poetry resemble prose—
Their argument they draw from godlike Marx.
All genres 'equal'! Each strand of his beard flows
Like hanging rope to strangle classic verse.

'Art for art's sake'; when politics is twined
With literature, its basic worth's denied.

A Sonnet on the Patriotic and Benevolent President of America, Donald John Trump

You are the harbinger of harmony,
In these tough times we supplicate to thee:
Save thou us from this viewless enemy,
Our mighty friend of highest pedigree.

You are the son incarnate of our Lord,
Whom He sends to redeem mankind this time
Like Jesus whom the fallen Man adored;
Your advent makes auspicious church-bells chime.

You promised us to punish evil powers,
Satanic knaves of cursèd Wuhan lab.
The world's sole star, the chosen king of ours,
May you protect us from the Chinese stab.

Let nasty hypocrites deride your way,
Your truthful voice reduces them to clay.

America, a Nightmare to the Director General of WHO, Tedros Adhanom, a Stooge of China

His accent's weird, his hair is pretty grey,
He is too calm to get into a fray.
His moustache bears the villainy of WHO,
His pompous mouth suppressed the Wuhan flu.
He talked of 'global solidarity',
But buttressed China in reality.
Three years ago he was elected chief,
In which crooked wise I shall relate in brief.
America and Canada did go
For British doctor David Nabarro,
While China's Xi like a foul magician
Installed this African politician,
To regulate the WHO at his command,
And give a scripted speech as he'd demand.
Besides the Wuhan plague he had concealed
Another plague in which thousands were killed.
It was an Ethiopian cholera,
He covered up that as a false chimera.
In him I see a misanthropic strain,
He loves to watch the plague-infected's pain.
He can be well compared to Beelzebub,
 A fallen devil who deserves our snub.
But his eternal friend is China's Xi,
A tyrant deft at stale conspiracy,
A modern Satan, who deceives mankind
To fall from God's grace which he did once find.
The more this dangerous friendship may grow,
The more diseased men soon will be laid low.
What is the fault man has committed now?
Not eating fruit, believing Tedros' vow.

His sweetened words in full deceptive vein
Cleaned up Xi's hand with Lady Macbeth's stain.
But who shall now redeem mankind this time,
And hail again the wholesome pristine clime?
Which country, which land, which blessed territory
Shall make us hale again and set us free?
American dream and nectar let us seek,
She will revive all men, diseased and weak.
Across the continents men sing of you,
And bid the Chinese products all adieu.
Your medicines and vaccines our world craves,
Best doctors are born west to Atlantic waves.
America, leader in the modern age,
You save the world from the communist rage.

A Sonnet on America's Humanitarian Move to Support the Protesters of Hong Kong, Threatened with the Imposition of a Sedition Law by the Chinese Communist Party

Seditions and revolts ought to be crushed,
When they surface in Marxist anarchy,
But those free Hong Kongers who have been hushed
By Chinese laws, deserve our amity.

America has spoken for their cause,
And preached a humanist gospel for them,
And championed freedom gaining world's applause;
This wealthy city China cannot claim.

How long will peaceful countries bear the frown
Of Beijing's leaders' harsh inhuman claims?
Their end is near; Washington holds the crown
Of blissful dawn, which for a new world aims.

No seeker of democracy should fear,
The White House holds its commie-killing-spear.

A Sonnet on Charlie Chase

(Charlie Chase is an 82-year-old veteran military officer and Trump supporter
from Massachusetts, assaulted for his political views last week)

Hail, good old man, we love your fortitude,
You served this nation with your holy brawn,
None can erode your steadfast rectitude,
Your glorious deeds shine like a blissful dawn.

O wise old countryman, your sinew's weak,
But once your strength had conquered farthest East,
Fleet time has failed to make your wisdom bleak,
That young assailant is a leftist beast.

Progressive liberals may injure you,
But deep in heart we pay you reverence,
The perpetrator certainly then knew
His every blow would spur wide resonance.

A true American's soul must have pined,
To see our soldier's image undermined.

A Sonnet on President Trump's Brilliant Decision to Terminate Relationship with WHO

A meagre forty million dollars' bribe
Is paid to regulate the WHO by China.
WHO serves them as an adulating scribe,
Oh what else can afford communist dogma!

President Trump, you rightfully withdrew
Relationship with such a flagrant group
That hides a pandemic and does not rue,
They are as murderous as a Maoist troop.

WHO knows well it's a tragic irony,
They are supposed to find for us a cure,
Instead, they work with Xi, our enemy,
And for mankind a sudden end ensure.

The prudent President has cleft the ties,
They should now stop to spread disease and lies.

How to be a Trendy Friend

Friendship is very common nowadays,
To be a friend one must know blabberings,
And show false kindness in most liberal ways
For animals and diverse human beings.

To enter college is an easy way
Of making lots of friends like herd of mares,
And rant on Lenin's deeds on any day,
For vodka revolution all he cares.

A rally on the climate change might aid
Your fame among the left progressive mates,

Their company makes faith in God to fade,
For that is what Lord Karl Marx truly hates.

If you are on a righteous moral track,
They will leave you out of their wanton team,
They frown on him who doesn't have a knack
For swinging rainbow sickles with a scream.

You have a chance to be their dearest friend,
If black cats wallow on your tattooed arms,
And costumes suit the latest insta-trend,
With piercings stuck somewhere that sounds alarms.

A march for social justice is not rare,
Like partying on the streets with body bare.
Retaining such friendship is tricky though,
Dissent is not allowed–Go with the flow!

Hunter Biden's Gallant Feats

(This poem is a satirical portrait of Joe Biden's son Hunter Biden's scandalous
private life, his affairs with his late brother Beau Biden's wife Hallie, South African
model Melissa Cohen and Lunden Roberts, with whom he had an illegitimate
child).

An adage says sons oft resemble dad,
Joe's son is, therefore, fed with father's art
Of courting ladies whether good or bad,
For, Hunter Biden hunts with honeyed heart.

Poor Beau, his brother, died of rare disease,
And Hunter wiped his grieving widow's tear,

Which from her nether eye she did release,
Little they mourned, but moaned so loud and sheer.

Meanwhile this widow's joys were temporal,
In state and partners Hunter hankers change,
Once cocaine robbed him job of an admiral,
Joe's proud of his deeds' wide eclectic range!

Indeed a great adventurer he is,
The queue of wenches following him proves this!

Liberal Artists

A little argument and then they hurt;
These liberals are so coy and sensitive.
They think they know all forms of decent art,
And claim consensus gives prerogative.
Their poetry requires subjective style
That craves an "I," a "me," a "my" or "mine."
Their views constrained to left side of the aisle
Require revolts of socialist design.
But oft their verse has splendid imagery,
Of camels flying high in azure sky,
Birds singing sweetly in a poetry...
As vapid as a tear a clown might cry.
For now, in colleges they reign supreme
All unaware here ends their Age's dream.

Obamagate: A Stark Reality

An old and covert crime of Democrats

Is brought before us by our President,
An evil game of deep-state bureaucrats
To slander Flynn, his friend and confidant.

Judge Sullivan, what made you fear and cease
Investigating, people know it all.
False accusations stole your midnight peace,
While secret crimes ensured Obama's fall.

A person born outside the mainland state,
Became a President and ruled our land.
His sabotage is called Obamagate,
Flynn was 'unmasked' to Russia as he planned.

The Democrats conspired in unknown ways,
And hid the biggest crime since Nixon's days.

Shi Zhengli, a Virologist at WIV, the Alleged Culprit behind the CCP Pandemic

Ambitious Shi, have you returned from France?
No longer we believe your spurious speech,
Your false research and your deceptive stance
On Wuhan plague that everywhere can reach.

Bat Woman of China, a curse on men,
Your deadly ventures claimed a million lives.
In Wuhan's lab you stored this pathogen,
Therein it grew and there it still revives.

Like Pandora you ruined humanity,
And filled this world with misery and woe.
Mean misanthrope, you sought divinity
Playing with a virus, our eternal foe!

Xi's party has always defended you,
The whole world hates you and will surely sue.

Tokens of Art

The cats are creatures of a liberal kind,
On jobless laps of artists, them we find.
And coffee too belongs to their domain,
More of a fashion than a drink certain.
This thing most certainly their purpose serves,
For looking more cool with multiple loves.
On weekends favourite haunts are costly pubs,
And Mondays saved for protests and hubbubs.
The causes have a wide and various range,
From human rights to underwear exchange.
But cleanliness on walls is not preferred,
Gobbledegooks as graffiti referred.
True artists fear to bash this nuisance now,
It's not allowed to raise a sane eyebrow.